MARIA HAD A LITTLE LLAMA

MARÍA TENÍA UNA LLAMITA

**Dedicated to all the Marias who
follow the beat of their own drum.**

Dedicado a todas las Marías que
siguen su proprio ritmo.

—Angela (María Navarrete) Dominguez

ISBN 978-0-545-67023-4

Copyright © 2013 by Angela Dominguez
All rights reserved. Published by Scholastic Inc., 557 Broadway, New York, NY 10012,
by arrangement with Henry Holt and Company, LLC.
SCHOLASTIC and associated logos are trademarks and/or registered trademarks of Scholastic Inc.

28 27 26 25 24   20 21 22 23 24/0

Printed in the U.S.A.   40
First Scholastic printing, January 2014

Designed by April Ward
Gouache and ink on Arches watercolor board were used to create the illustrations of this book.

MARIA HAD A LITTLE LLAMA
MARÍA TENÍA UNA LLAMITA

ANGELA DOMINGUEZ

SCHOLASTIC INC.

Maria had a little llama

María tenía una llamita

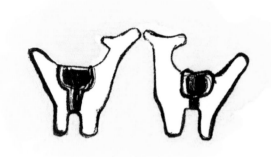

**whose fleece was
white as snow.**

cuya lana era tan
blanca como la nieve.

And everywhere that Maria went,

Y a donde María iba,

the llama was sure to go.

la llama la seguía.

She followed Maria to school one day.

Un día siguió a María a la escuela.

It made the children laugh and play
to see a llama at school.

Los niños rieron y jugaron
al ver una llama en la escuela.

The teacher had to send her out.

La maestra tuvo que mandarla afuera.

**But still she lingered near
and waited patiently about . . .**

Pero ella se quedó cerca
esperando pacientemente...

. . . for Maria to appear!

¡a que apareciera María!

"Why does the llama love Maria so?"
the eager children cried.
"Maria loves the llama, you know,"
the teacher did reply.

—¿Por qué la llama quiere tanto a María?
—preguntaron ansiosamente los niños.
—Porque María quiere mucho a la llama
—la maestra respondió.

The End

Fin